I0451242

Operation: Rebirth

Felix Davila

Copyright © 2013 by Felix Davila

ISBN: 978-0-578-13269-3

<u>Acknowledgments</u>

First and foremost, I want to thank God. With Him all things are possible.

I want to give a special thanks to my mother, Lisa Colon, we've been through a whole lot, and she has always been my light in my darkest moments. I know I was a handful as a child, but my mother made sure I was always on the right path to becoming a better person and I love her for that.

I'd like to shed some love for my two siblings, Francisco Pena and Crystal Pena, two of the best people I've had the privilege to be raised with.

And a huge thank-you for those who have supported my endeavors.

<u>Timeline</u>: Gulf War

<u>Characters</u>:

Sergeant Marcus White

Corporal Calvin Smalls

Private First Class Charles Anderson

Private Brandon Walker

Private Francis Peña

Private Theodore "The Tank" Bronson

Private Edward Hawkins

Private Andy Chen

<u>Prologue</u>

Army Base in Kuwait City

1400 hours

A group of army soldiers lounged by the corridors of the United States Army base in Kuwait City. Both Sergeant Marcus White and Corporal Calvin Smalls approached the soldiers.

"It says here that there are six of you in my brigade but I only see five," Marcus White barked, pointing at his clipboard.

Private Brandon Walker jogged out of the entrance doorway to the base to where the army men were located.

"I'm here, Sir. Private Brandon Walker, reporting for duty."

"Good to see you made it," White replied sarcastically.

"Listen up, men. I am Sergeant Marcus White and this is Corporal Calvin

Smalls. My superiors for this mission handpicked you all. Personally, looking at your credentials I would have probably chosen otherwise. As of now, the details of our mission have not yet been divulged to me, but what I was told is that we must head to a small town south of here called Hafar Al Batin, and we will be updated about our mission when we are halfway there. I lead a tight-knit unit, and I expect everyone to follow my orders. At our disposal we have several vehicles and a decent amount of supplies to cover our mission. Any questions?"

The army men answered in sync: "No, Sir."

"Then load up, we leave in an hour."

Chapter I

Outside of Al-Jahra

1900 hours

"All I can think to myself as I sit in the passenger side of this Hummer is that I can't believe this shit is happening to me. All I wanted was a steady paycheck and as soon as I decide to join the army, a war starts!"

"Are you daydreaming over there, Private Walker?"

Private Brandon Walker, newly recruited, was an underprivileged young African American from the Bronx. Private Walker sat beside Private First Class Charles Anderson. Anderson, a roughneck from Texas with a tattoo of the Confederate flag on his arm and a grade-A dickhead, was known to be a bit of a racist, and got under the newly recruit's skin ever since Anderson was demoted for not following orders, leaving one private with a wounded shoulder from a Iraqi extremist.

"No, Sir. Just thinking to myself, nothing more," replied Walker.

"So where are you from, private?" Anderson followed up with another question.

"I'm from the Bronx, New York, Sir."

"Oh. So you're one of those Bronx bombers that like to graffiti trains and other people's property, huh?" Anderson said with a grin.

"No, Sir. You have me confused with someone else. Where are you from?"

"I'm from good ole' Texas, where everything is big, except for them Mexicans crossing those borders," Anderson replied with laughter.

"*Come in. This is Sergeant Marcus White.*" The walkie-talkie went off, interrupting the awkward conversation.

"*We are entering a small village called Al-Jahra. We will set up camp there and will continue to Hafar Al Batin at 700 hours, over.*"

"Roger that, Sergeant," Anderson replied.

—

"What a shitty place. Right, *papi*?" shouted Private Francis Peña over the roaring engine of the M2 Bradley.

The M2 Bradley is a preferred pick of vehicles for the United States Army, covered with armor-plated steel with a top speed of 45 miles per hour due to its weight of 30 tons. But what the M2 Bradley lacks in speed it makes up with its artillery. Its primary weapon is a 25-millimeter M242 chain gun capable of spitting out 900 rounds in under a minute and a half. Its secondary weapon is a 7.62-millimeter M240-caliber machine gun with a monstrous 2,000 rounds at its disposal. This beast can rip a small infantry apart, and Private Theodore "the Tank" Bronson loved every inch of it.

"Definitely is, my Spanish compadre," replied Bronson.

Private Francis Peña, born and raised in a broken home in the ghettos of South Central, California, had been the best of friends with Private Bronson since boot camp. They were known as the "odd couple," the yin and yang. Peña was five foot nine, Puerto Rican, and of medium build, and Bronson, six foot five, 250 pounds of muscle. Bronson, born and bred in Boston, Massachusetts, to parents who migrated from England, was the star of his high school wrestling team. He had the persona of a hard rocker, with a mohawk, barbwire tattoo on his ripped biceps, and a black bandana that hung from his belt loop. Bronson was one not to cross paths with, and Private Peña knew this and used it to his advantage. Peña was known to have a grotesque sense of humor and Bronson was always there to back him up if trouble were to come Peña's way.

"This M2 is really cramped. I can't even move in here. What's with all this crap in here if we have a supply truck— really? Why are there tubes of toothpaste falling out this box?" complained Bronson.

"Well just be glad it isn't Chinese toothpaste. That's been banned from every country on this planet," laughed Private Peña.

"FUCK YOU!" yelled Private Andy Chen.

Chen had always been at the top of his class. Chen, was the only child and of parents who had migrated from China with high aspirations for him to be a mathematician. He always did everything he could to upset his father, listening to his favorite rap group, the Wu-Tang Clan, until late in the evening, even getting their "Wu" logo tattooed on his arm. What really did it for his father was when he enrolled in the army rather than pursuing his father's ambitions for him. Now he was the convoy's communications expert.

"Relax, I was only kidding," smirked Peña.

"Well at least I wasn't raised in an apartment with forty of my other relatives stacked up like sardines," Private Chen joked.

"Shut up, we're here. Get out," yelled Bronson.

Al-Jahra
2000 hours

Private Edward Hawkins jumped out of the six-wheel supply truck, which carried the convoy's supplies, food, and extra weapons and ammunition. Hawkins, being the son of retired Edward Hawkins Sr., knew everything about firearms and how to configure just about every handheld weapon in the United States Army. He had always been the shortest among his peers, and in this brigade it was no different. Standing tall at five foot two and weighing in at 140 pounds, he was a strong, courageous son of a bitch. Being from Baltimore, Maryland, Hawkins grew tough skin standing toe to toe with anyone who disrespected him.

"Shouldn't there be a rope for you to climb down that truck, Eddie?" Private Peña jokingly asked.

"Are we going to hear this clown open his trap the whole mission?" responded Hawkins.

"GET IN FORMATION, SOLDIERS!" screamed Corporal Calvin Smalls. Corporal Smalls was known to be a straight shooter and had been by the sergeant's side for several years now. Born and raised in Newark, New Jersey, he found his escape in the United States Army. He left behind his pregnant wife and financial problems, which he preferred to keep to himself.

One after the other the soldiers stood in line formation, bodies as stiff as a flagpole. Corporal Calvin Smalls could have been a drill sergeant the way he commanded the soldiers. No one moved, waiting for the next set of orders.

"At ease, soldiers," requested Sergeant White stepping out from the backseat of the front Hummer.

Sergeant White had been in the service for 15 years. Born and raised on the cruel streets of Detroit, Michigan, Marcus White developed a no tolerance reputation, and was one of the Army's most distinguished active sergeants.

"I will bring everyone up to speed within the hour. Set up camp," ordered Sergeant White.

Sergeant White, looking down at his clipboard, called out to Private Hawkins.

"I hear you're somewhat of a weapons expert. I want a full inventory of our weapons and ammo. Something tells me we may have company soon, and I want to be prepared if we get into any kind of trouble."

"Yes, Sir." Hawkins replied, saluted, and went straight to inventorying the firearms on the supply truck.

"And Private Anderson: find out if the locals are friendly or hostile. We don't need anyone shooting us in the back."

"Sir! That's Private First Class Anderson, Sir!" replied Anderson.

"Excuse me?"

"Sir, I'm a pay grade higher than a private, Sir," answered Anderson

"I don't give a damn if you're picking up camel shit, private. When I give an order I don't need to be reminded what rank I'm talking to. Are we going to have a problem here, private?" White said with a stern voice.

"Sir, no, Sir. Right away, Sir." Private First Class Anderson replied and power walked toward the nearest civilian.

"Can you believe this prick, corporal? If he gives me a hard time, I'm shooting him in the shoulder myself," White said with a straight face.

—

"Christ it's hot out here!" complained Peña.

"What did you expect? We're in the middle of the desert, genius," Bronson responded while carrying ammunition crates out of the M2 Bradley.

"Why couldn't we have been placed somewhere on a beach, with beautiful women feeding us grapes." Peña was fantasizing.

"Well that sounds real peachy right now." Bronson wiped the sweat from his brow.

—

"Brandon, right?" asked Chen.

"Yup, Brandon Walker," Brandon replied.

"Give me a hand with these crates."

"So what's your story Brandon?"

"Story?"

"Yeah. Why did you join the army out of all things to do? Why come to this wasteland?" asked Chen.

"Well, where I'm from you either make money the right way or the wrong way. So I chose to join the army. But if I knew two months before I joined there would be a war, I may have chosen another route. So what's your reason, Chen?"

"I joined out of spite to my folks. I've always been forced to study hard and follow my father's dreams of me being a mathematician. So instead I joined the army and—let me tell you—my father was pissed," Chen laughed. "Now I run communications for this convoy."

—

"LISTEN, YOU IRAQI FUCK! I DON'T UNDERSTAND ONE WORD YOU'RE SAYING!" yelled Anderson.

"Look at this idiot." Hawkins was pointing toward Charles Anderson and an Iraqi villager arguing.

"Are you hiding weapons in your village? Tell me before I pistol-whip the shit out of you," continued Anderson.

Grabbing the turban off the civilian's head, Anderson, again verbally abusing the civilian asked, "Are you hiding a gun under here!?"

"Private! What the hell do you think you're doing?" asked Sergeant White.

"I'm trying to get intel out of this civilian, Sir," replied Anderson.

"Well it's obvious he doesn't understand you, go make yourself useful and help Private Hawkins with inventory."

———

As the troops set up shop, the villagers watched with excitement and paranoia. Whispers in an unfamiliar language surrounded the army men. As the sun clocked out to retire for the day, the night took its place as the men encircled the campfire, eating rations and awaiting further instructions from their Sergeant, Marcus White.

"Listen up, men," spoke Sergeant Marcus White. "I have been informed about the details of our mission. I received word from headquarters that we are to rendezvous with an Abdul Hakeem in Hafar Al Batin at 0700 hours. I was informed that Mr. Hakeem has valuable intel and we are to retrieve it. We are to expect hostiles in the area."

"This is a grab-and-go mission," Corporal Calvin Smalls continued. "We will sleep in shifts. I want a spotter and marksman on top of one of these buildings. We will then head to Hafar Al Batin at daybreak."

"Now that Corporal Smalls and I have filled you men in with the details, anyone have any questions?" Sergeant White asked.

"Yes, I have one," Private Hawkins replied. "What can we expect with the hostiles weaponry?"

"We can expect fully automatic weapons, nothing we can't handle. Any other questions?" There was a pause. "I'll take the silence as an indication that there are no further questions then. As you were, gentlemen."

Al-Jahra
0400 hours

"Oh man, I'm sleepy," Hawkins yawned.

"I know what you mean, brother," Walker replied, tiredly.

"What time is it, Brandon?"

"It's four in the morning. Sun should be coming up soon."

"Well I'm going to rest my eyes for a minute. Looks like I won't be testing out this M25 sniper rifle tonight. Wake me up in thirty minutes, Brandon."

As the night slowly came to a close, Brandon began to slowly drift off. Laying across from him out cold, Private Edward Hawkins gripped his M25 sniper rifle as if it were the last bottle of Scotch on this dreadful rock. Looking down from the two-story building, Private Walker could see his fellow brothers-in-arms sleeping by the campfire, the village as quiet as the desert breeze. Brandon's eyes began to wander, slowly examining the three two-story buildings that surrounded his comrades. Brandon's eyes, scanning window to window as he fought with all his willpower to keep them from closing, embarked on a particular window on the second floor of the building farthest east from where his comrades slept. A man standing by the window starring at Brandon gave a cold chill down his spine. Both Brandon and the unknown man's eyes met.

A moan from Hawkins made Brandon shift his eyes at Hawkins's body turning over. Brandon shifted his eyes back toward the window but the man had disappeared behind the curtains. This encounter gave Brandon an eerie feeling. Pondering at what had just happened, Brandon shifted his body back toward the open terrain and saw headlights in the distance. He grabbed his binoculars and adjusted his view toward the oncoming vehicles on the same road he and his convoy had arrived from earlier. One… two… three… four… five vehicles, Brandon counted. Watching patiently as the vehicles continued toward Hafar Al Batin, Brandon hoped they would bypass the village.

Suddenly he saw three vehicles break out of formation and start to drive down the road toward the camp.

"Oh shit. Wake up, Hawkins. We have company." Walker shook Hawkins's leg.

"What happened? Where?"

"They're on your six. I doubt they're friendlies."

"Get Sergeant on the radio, Brandon. We may have trouble."

"Come in, sergeant. We have company. Three unidentified vehicles inbound. Waiting on further instructions."

"*Copy that, private. If they become hostile, fire at will. Over,*" Sergeant White replied over the radio.

"This may get interesting Brandon, grab that M249 machine gun over there. If they act up give em' hell," Hawkins demanded.

———

"Listen up, men. We have potential hostiles inbound. Lock and load, gentlemen.

Peña and Bronson: I want you two on the far east building. Anderson and Chen: take the west. Corporal Smalls and I will cover the north side of the building where Privates Hawkins and Walker are. Put out that campfire. Do not shoot unless fired upon. You have your orders. Now move out!" barked Sergeant White.

—

"*Ay Dios*. Time to get this party started," Peña said while loading his assault rifle.

"It's about time we get some action. Guess this wasn't a dull ride after all," Bronson added as he kicked sand onto the campfire to put it out.

"Hope Chen and Anderson are ready, too. This may be a long night," implied Peña.

—

"I hope you shoot better than your people drive, Chen," Anderson suggested.

"I got your back. Just make sure you follow orders. I'm not in the mood to get shot in the shoulder tonight," replied Chen.

"Here they come!" Walker said over the radio.

Three white pickup trucks covered in a heavy layer of dirt pulled into the center of the village. Men jumped off the back of the trucks with guns drawn and circled their vehicles as if they were waiting for someone or something. Then a radio from within one of their vehicles went off. One of the men reached for it and answered. After some exchange of words the man stepped forward.

"I know you're hiding, you filthy Americans. I want to speak to your leader," said the Iraqi.

Sergeant White stepped out from the side of the building.

"I am Sergeant Marcus White of the United States Army. So you speak English. Who are you and what do you want?"

"I am Ishmael Salem and I am here to kick you out of my country. You and your men will put your weapons down and come with me."

"Well I'm afraid we can't do that Mr. Salem. We are here on an important mission and cannot leave with you. We are not looking for any trouble."

"You now have trouble, Mr. White. You come to my country and demand like we are no people. You come and shoot my people. You have trouble now," said Salem, angrily.

——

"*We have trouble, fifteen hostiles. No one fires until Sergeant is clear. Is that understood? Hawkins, keep an eye on Salem*," said Corporal Smalls over the radio.

"I have Salem reaching for something," Walker said over the walkie-talkie.

"It's a pistol!" screamed Anderson.

"*Bring him down, Hawkins*," Smalls ordered.

A loud popping noise echoed from the rifle of Private Hawkins. The bullet pierced the skull of Salem and his body fell face first into the sandy ground, starting a firefight that would certainly end with more dead.

——

"GET DOWN, SERGEANT!" screamed Smalls.

Sergeant Marcus White dove underneath the Hummer, pistol drawn.

"OPEN FIRE!" yelled Sergeant White on the walkie-talkie.

An exchange of fire lit up the desert night sky. Private Hawkins continued to fire on the unexpected hostiles, one after another taking direct hits from the M25 sniper rifle. On the far east side, Private Peña shot recklessly at hostiles who managed to shield themselves behind their pickup truck.

"Take this and a little of that you filthy *putas*!" screamed trigger-happy Peña.

"Control your shots, Francis, you're not shooting anything," suggested Bronson.

"*Toma*, I got one of them!"

"Good, now try and keep up. Follow me."

Private Bronson kicked in the side door of the building with Peña right behind him, both men moving as quickly as possible room to room with guns at the ready. Bronson kicked open another door to find an Iraqi woman hunched over her husband, screaming. The man had been shot in the chest from the exchange of fire outside, dead. A casualty of war.

"*Peña and Bronson, get over here, now,*" Smalls said over the radio.

"On our way," Bronson replied.

——

On the far west side of the village, both Anderson and Chen had their hands full with three hostiles who had managed to hide behind their vehicle.

"Cover me," Chen demanded.

Private Anderson opened fire at the three hostiles. Chen ran and dove by the passenger side of the supply truck, then crawled underneath the truck to see a clear view of two of the hostiles' legs behind the pickup truck. Chen opened fire at their shins and the hostiles immediately fell to the ground, grasping their legs. Chen then finished them off with shots to the sternum. The remaining hostile of the three saw Chen underneath the truck and opened fire, bullets just barely missing him impacted the ground beside him. Dust and debris covered Chen. Chen rolled over to his right to hide behind the front tire. The enraged hostile jumped up from his cover and shot at the front tire, deflating it. Anderson opened fire again taking out the hostile with two bullets to the chest and one to the stomach.

Pulling up Chen by his forearm, Anderson said with satisfaction, "That's some good thinking Chen, guess you do shoot better than you drive."

—

"What the hell are you doing Walker!? SHOOT!" screamed Hawkins.

Walker, frozen with fear gripping the M249 machine gun, said, "I never shot anyone before. I'm not made for this!"

"Man the fuck up and SHOOT! There are eight of us and seven of them!"

Brandon, scared out of his skin, opened the tripod of the M249 machine gun and rested the gun on the ledge of the two-story building.

"SQUEEZE THE FUCKING TRIGGER!" barked Hawkins.

Brandon, a novice to the battlefield, pulled the trigger. Shell after shell firing directly into the gas tank of the pickup truck, which created a small explosion that killed the four hostiles hiding behind it instantly, while injuring the remaining three.

"Apprehend the last three men. Bronson, get Sergeant now!" ordered Smalls.

Privates Peña, Anderson, and Chen ran out toward the three injured hostiles lying on the ground. The privates went directly toward the hostiles' weapons, kicking them away from their reach and pointing their automatic weapons at the hostile heads.

"*NO SE MUEVEN*, MOTHERFUCKERS!" screamed Peña.

"Let's go, sergeant. We have three hostiles by the wreckage. We are waiting on your orders, Sir," Bronson informed Sergeant White while helping him to his feet.

The eight army men surrounded the three hostiles, weapons resting at their chests. The hostiles looked exhausted and battered. One hostile farthest to the right and nearest to the explosion was in complete agony. After losing one of his limbs in the explosion, he was slowly dying a painful death. The middle hostile had two bullet holes in the upper region of his left shoulder.

"Who blew up the truck?" Bronson asked.

"That recognition goes to Walker" Hawkins answered.

"Fucking A, brother. I couldn't have done it better myself." Bronson gave Walker a thumbs up.

"So what are we going to do with these three, sergeant?" asked Walker.

"I want you and Anderson to put this poor fellow out of his misery. Private Chen and Bronson, tie up these two. I want answers as to how they found us," replied White.

"Walker, grab an arm and I'll grab the other. Help me drag his ass into that building so we can finish him off," asked Anderson.

Privates Anderson and Walker grabbed hold of the hostile's arms and began to drag him to the building on the west side of the village. Privates Bronson and Chen sat the remaining hostiles upright, tying their arms behind their backs with zip ties. Bronson, as strong as he was, grabbed the wrists of one hostile and lifted him to his feet nearly breaking his arm. Chen did the same with his captured hostile. Privates Bronson and Chen then faced the prisoners toward Sergeant White and Corporal Smalls.

"What do you want? How did you know we were here? Where are your other friends?" asked Sergeant White.

The questions asked were answered with an angry stare at the sergeant. The hostile Bronson tied up said something in Arabic and spat in the sergeant's face. Bronson, without hesitation, placed his hand on the hostile's wounded left shoulder and began to squeeze tighter and tighter. The hostile fell to his knees screaming in agonizing pain.

Wiping his face, White said, "Well it seems to me you're not willing to talk, but you will answer my questions one way or another."

———

Privates Walker and Anderson laid the hostile against the wall on the first floor of the building. Anderson pulled out his pistol, cocked the hammer back, and passed it to Walker.

"Here you go Mr. Save-the-Day. Time to finish your handy work," said Anderson.

"I don't feel comfortable executing someone."

"It's not execution if the guy's dying already. Forget it, I'll do it," Anderson said while grabbing the gun from Walker's hand.

Anderson crouched down and placed the muzzle on the hostile's chest and squeezed the trigger. *BANG!* The hostile slouched over and was finally put out of his misery. Several moments later, a loud *pop*, which sounded like a gunshot, followed by a scream came from outside. Anderson and Walker ran out the door back to where the rest of the squad was waiting.

—

"AH, FUCK! I've been shot!" screamed Peña.

"Everyone take cover!" ordered Sergeant White.

"Did anyone see where the shot came from!?" asked Smalls.

"Where were you shot?" asked Chen.

"On my right arm," answered Peña.

"It's just a flesh wound. You're alive. Stop being such a pussy," said Bronson.

"Well it hurt," replied Peña.

POP! Another shot was fired in the direction of the army men.

"It's coming from the second floor of the building on the east side," said Hawkins, pointing in the direction the shot came from.

"It's the same guy I saw earlier starring at me," Private Walker said to himself.

"Bronson, Walker, and Hawkins: Take the west wing of the building.

Anderson and Smalls: On my six. We will
take the east wing. Chen: Remain here.
Patch up Peña and look after the hostiles.
Everyone move out," Sergeant White
ordered.

———

Bronson, followed by Walker and
Hawkins, were the first to arrive at the
building.

"Prepare for entry." Bronson took
the lead.

Walker posted on the left side of the
door and Hawkins took the right, guns
drawn. Bronson kicked the door clean off.
Bronson, scanning the area with his
automatic weapon, signaled it was clear.
Seconds later Sergeant White, Anderson,
and Smalls regrouped at their location.
Sergeant White took point and carefully led
the squad up the stairs. The squad found
three locked doors, and the hostile could be
in any one of them. Sergeant White signaled
to Bronson and Hawkins to take the door to
the left, and Anderson and Walker to take
the door to the right. Sergeant White and
Smalls took the middle door. White signaled

with his hand a count of three. *One… two…
three…* The troops kicked all three doors
open simultaneously. Bronson and Hawkins
looked in: no hostile. Anderson and Walker:
same result. White and Anderson: a different
result. The hostile had a pistol in one hand
and a walkie-talkie in the other.

"Put the gun down now!" screamed
Sergeant White drawing his weapon at the
newly acquainted hostile.

"You won't take me. You Americans
are the devil," screamed the hostile.

The hostile raised his pistol to his
head.

"Wait!" screamed Smalls.

"Here I come, Allah," whispered the
hostile and pulled the trigger.

Pieces of brain tissue and blood
painted the wall and the hostile's limp body
hit the floor with a loud thump. The walkie-
talkie rolled to the foot of Sergeant White.

Sergeant White crouched down and
picked up the walkie-talkie. "This is
probably how they knew we were here. It's
time to go."

—

The sky began to fill with shades of orange and yellow, signaling the morning's arrival.

"Time to load up, men. Bronson, put the two prisoners in one of the Hummers. It looks like this area has been compromised. It will not get any easier from here on out," White said.

"Sarge, you're right about that. Our supply truck has been hit. The front tire is out, and we're shit out of luck with a spare," said Hawkins.

"Okay, so grab what you can and load the two Hummers and the Bradley. We leave in thirty."

Chapter II

Outside of Al-Jahra
0700 hours

After a long night of resistance the convoy left with two prisoners minus a vehicle. Sergeant White, Corporal Smalls, and Private Walker rode in the front Hummer followed by Private First Class Anderson and Private Hawkins with the two prisoners in the backseat of the second Hummer. Privates Bronson, Chen, and Peña followed in the M2 Bradley. Leaving behind their supply truck due to an exchange of fire, the squad now had less than 50 percent of its ammunition, weapons, and rations.

"Come in, headquarters. We are currently forty miles from Hafar Al Batin. We have encountered hostiles sooner than expected. We have apprehended two hostiles, and they are currently in our custody. Requesting an extraction point for the two prisoners. Over," Sergeant White requested over the Hummer radio.

"Negative, Sergeant White. We currently do not have anyone in the area for an extraction of your prisoners. Over," replied headquarters.

"Looks like we have no choice but to carry the extra baggage," White said to Smalls.

"Well I don't see the need to have them with us, sergeant. We are down on our rations and supplies over the nonsense they caused," said Smalls.

"I do see your point, Calvin, but they may have some intel on the whereabouts of their friends."

"They may be expecting us, sergeant," suggested Walker.

"Which is why we will be entering guns at the ready, avoiding any casualties," replied White.

—

The convoy continued on the road to Hafar Al Batin. As the sun began to inch above the sandy mountains in the distance and illuminate the memorizing golden landscape, small goat farms began to appear on either side on the road. Small goat herds, shepherded by bearded men dressed from head to toe kept a focused eye on the unfamiliar armored vehicles that entered unannounced on their lands.

"What I wouldn't give for a cold beer right about now," Bronson said, wishfully.

"A full night's sleep sounds much better than that beer," replied Chen, slurring his words.

"How's the arm, brother?" Bronson asked while squeezing Peña's wound, jokingly.

"Ahh! It still hurts you idiot," yelled Peña, removing Bronson's arm forcefully.

"You lucky that fool didn't shoot you in that big ass head of yours," laughed Bronson.

—

The two prisoners sitting in the backseat sat quietly. The prisoner sitting directly behind Anderson stared fiercely at the rearview mirror into Anderson's eyes.

The other prisoner gazed at the upcoming goat farm with a smirk on his battered face.

"If this fuck doesn't stop staring at me while I'm driving I'll have to put my boot in his ass," Anderson barked.

"I think he likes you," Hawkins said sarcastically.

"And what the hell this camel face fuck is smirking at?"

As soon as those words left Anderson's lips, a rocket buzzed above the hood of the Hummer, missing it by mere inches. The rocket collided with the ground 20 feet from its target. In the midst of confusion and nervousness, Anderson swerved the Hummer right into a ditch.

———

"Contact! We are under attack. There's a hostile with a grenade launcher on your three. Right in the goat farm!" yelled Hawkins on the radio.

"Copy that, private," Sergeant White replied. "Chen, take that son of bitch out!"

"My pleasure, Sir," replied Chen.

"Bronson, jump on the gunner and take that prick out!" ordered Chen.

Bronson lifted the ceiling hatch and grabbed hold of the M242 chain gun. He cocked the weapon and squeezed the trigger in the direction of the goat farm, the non-discriminate bullets hitting everything in sight, shredding through stone and goat flesh, exiting the chain gun barrel—massive ammunition traveling at a thousand meters per second. The shell casings rained into the interior of the Bradley. Goats scattering in all directions fearing the wrath of the Bradley's M242 chain gun left the concealed hostile revealed to the Bradley's fury. Out in the open and with no place to hide, the hostile began to run toward the watering well 20 meters from his position.

"Don't let him go!" screamed Peña.

Bronson turned the M242 chain gun toward the direction in which the hostile was running. Slugs hitting the ground behind the hostile left small craters as if miniature land mines were exploding after every step the hostile took. The hostile leaped behind the well just barely dodging the tsunami of bullets behind him. Bronson continued on with the onslaught of bullets tearing away at the stone watering well, stone after stone falling off as if Bronson were purposely toying with the hostile.

"Hold your fire!" yelled Chen, slapping at Bronson's leg.

The hostile then slumped over the side of what was left of the watering well. Smoke and dust elevated off the ground and left with a hurry as the wind blew by.

"That's some serious firing power," laughed Peña.

"Definitely is, brother," replied Bronson.

▬

The Hummer that Anderson and Hawkins were in lay rested in a ditch.

"You alright?" asked Anderson.

"Yea, I'm good," replied Hawkins.

"Let's get out of here and back on the road."

▬

"Listen up, Chen. Check the area, and make sure there aren't any other surprises from our friends," ordered Sergeant White.

Chen steered the Bradley off the road toward the goat farm in the direction the rocket came from. Goat corpses covered the sandy ground beneath them. Chen stopped the vehicle and Bronson and Peña exited to scan the area.

"Shit, Bronson. Did you even try to avoid shooting the goats?" asked Peña.

"They should have never been in the way in the first place," replied Bronson.

"I thought Sarge said these guys only had, at the most, automatic weapons. Didn't expect to be dodging rockets out here."

"I'm not going to underestimate these people, Francis, and I think you shouldn't either. You have a bullet in your arm as proof."

"Look at this poor fellow. Sucks to be him," Peña said while trying to hide his smirk.

The hostile lay motionless. The bullet from the M242 chain gun left a hole the size of a golf ball in the hostile's chest. The grenade launcher had suffered the same fate from the Bradley's main weaponry and was deemed useless.

"Let's go. Time to move out," yelled Chen from the Bradley.

Bronson and Peña jumped back onto the Bradley and they rendezvoused back with the rest of convoy. Bronson sat on top of the Bradley staring at what used to be a goat farm. Piles of goat flesh littered the ground. The carnage looked as if these poor animals went through a butcher shop.

———

"It seems the hostiles in this area are determined to stop us, Sir," said Walker.

"Yes it seems that way," replied Sergeant White.

"Permission to speak freely, Sir."

"I encourage it, Private Walker."

"What does the military find so important about this intel that they sent us into harm's way with little detail about the mission? Because since we set course to retrieve this intel we have been under constant fire since we arrived in this dreadful place."

"Well honestly, private, I have not been informed of any additional details except to meet with Abdul Hakeem and return highly valuable intel back to base."

"Well I guess our government has been a little off on sharing vital information, considering the fact our enemies have grenade launchers. There's no way to even know what else is waiting for us in that town."

"You are correct, Walker, which is why we must be prepared for anything and everything."

—

"I should shoot you in your fucking face!" yelled Anderson. "Because of you two we almost was blown to shit. Hawkins, cover up their faces. I'm sick of them looking at me."

Hawkins turned over and faced the two hostiles behind him. He then lifted the front bottom half of their shirts over their heads. Anderson then asked Hawkins to grab the wheel, and Anderson turned quickly and punched the hostile directly behind him right in the face and returned to steering the vehicle.

"That's for staring at me," Anderson sneered.

Outside of Hafar Al Batin
1200 Hours

The convoy continued along the road toward the town of Hafar Al Batin. The town was within eyesight and the sun, reaching its peak, suggested it was about noon. Sergeant White grabbed his walkie-talkie and began talking into it.

"Listen, men. We are near Hafar Al Batin. We are to meet with Abdul Hakeem, pick up the intel, and hightail it out of there. This is a grab-and-go, so the sooner we get this done, the sooner we get home. I assume there will be resistance, considering the welcome party last night. So lock and load, men."

In sync, all the troops began loading up on ammunition, checking their weapons, and reassuring each other's body armor. Bronson loaded the M242 with its massive ammunition. Chen opened the grenade crate and handed Bronson and Peña what they could carry. Hawkins checked and rechecked his rifle. Walker loaded the M249 assault rifle with a new magazine and took care in adjusting his body armor. Sergeant White took out his side arm, a Beretta M9, and loaded the pistol with a fresh magazine. The convoy began closing in on Hafar Al Batin. The small town—no wider than a mile in all directions, with buildings no higher than three stories—was in full view. The convoy has finally reached its destination with no casualties.

Chapter III

Town of Hafar Al Batin
1300 hours

The convoy pulled up to the center of town. Three-story buildings made up the circumference of the small town as if enclosed by stone walls. A water tower at the very edge of the town hydrated the residents. A statue of a woman and child marked the town's center. The population of approximately 150 people lived in this encircled area. With no visible vegetation in the town, the main source of nourishment was from farmers' markets in distant towns.

The townspeople stared, as if disgusted with the sight of outsiders. Women clutched their children between their arms as if scared someone might snatch up the only thing of value in their lives. With eager eyes, the residents looked on as the soldiers stepped outside of their vehicles. One after another, the army men made the residents well aware of their presence, as if they were Spartans entering the Roman Coliseum for battle.

"Where is our contact, Sir?" asked Smalls.

"I was told he'll show his face at the sight of our uniform," replied White.

"Look." Walker pointed at a man walking toward them.

A full-bearded man holding a briefcase stepped out from behind a building column and began walking eagerly toward the convoy. The man stopped in front of the eight army men with worried eyes.

"Which one of you is Sergeant Marcus White?" asked the bearded man.

"That would be me. Are you our contact?" Sergeant White asked, in turn.

"I am Dr. Abdul Hakeem, a biochemist. My organization and your government have been in close contact for some time."

"What is your organization? And why are we here?"

"That is classified, I was told to hand this briefcase over to you as soon as possible."

"Do you know the contents of this briefcase?" questioned White.

"The contents cannot be discussed. It is confidential. I have also been given strict instructions to tell you about the delivery of the briefcase. It is never to be open and it is to be delivered straight to your superiors. The contents of this briefcase are of the upmost importance."

"Understood," replied White.

Abdul Hakeem pulled out a key from his side jacket pocket and began to fiddle with the handcuffs that had bound him to the briefcase. The handcuffs opened with a *click* and fell to the ground. Dr. Hakeem handed the briefcase over to Sergeant White.

A buzzing sound was the only thing Sergeant White could hear as he stared in shock into Abdul Hakeem's eyes as they rolled into the back of his head. Blood smeared Sergeant White's uniform as a bullet exited the temporal lobe of Dr.

Hakeem. Hakeem was dead before hitting the ground.

"Sniper! Everyone take cover now!" yelled Hawkins.

The convoy scattered to take cover. Chen, Peña, and Smalls jumped behind the front Hummer. Bronson, Anderson, and Hawkins took to the nearest building, and Sergeant White and Walker hid behind the statue.

—

"Did anyone see where the shot came from?" yelled White from across the yard.

"No but it had to come from higher ground," answered Chen.

"Get to the roof and fish him out, Hawkins," ordered White over the walkie-talkie.

"Already on my way up, Sarge," replied Hawkins.

Hawkins ran up the flights of stairs skipping steps on the way up. He nudged the door that led to the roof and removed his rifle from its shoulder strap. Hawkins then crouched down and made his way to the ledge, placing the tripod on the ledge. He began scanning the area through the rifle's scope. Scanning building after building, rooftop after rooftop, there was no sniper in sight. Hawkins finally made his way to the top of the water tower. The sun reflecting off of the rifles scope gave up the sniper's position. Hawkins adjusted the scope for a greater distance, checked the wind force, and aimed the barrel of the rifle at the sniper's nose. Without hesitation, Hawkins squeezed the trigger. The sniper round gobbled up the distance between Hawkins and the sniper with incredible speed and nearly decapitated the sniper.

"He's down, Sir," Hawkins informed Sergeant White.

—

An unexpected barrage of automatic weapon fire echoed in the courtyard. A large brigade of hostiles from all directions began to move in on the convoy. The convoy lay behind cover. An endless shower of automatic weapons prevented any movement. Chen reached into his pouch and pulled out a grenade.

"As soon as this goes off haul ass into the building behind us. We are sitting ducks if we don't move from this position. I'll cover you from here."

Chen pulled the pin from the grenade and chucked it toward the nearest hostiles. The four hostiles nearest to the grenade had no chance of escaping the blast of shrapnel. Chen leaned over the hood of the Hummer and gave covering fire to Peña and Smalls. Both Peña and Smalls ran in a crouching position toward the building.

——

"Hawkins, how many hostiles do you see!?" barked White.

"I count seventeen, Sir," Hawkins answered while pulling the trigger, taking down another hostile.

"Correction, Sir, sixteen."

"Continue taking them out, private," replied White.

"We need someone on that gunner!" screamed Anderson over the walkie.

"Do we have someone near the Bradley?" White said over the walkie.

"I am, Sir, but I'm pinned down by all this fire. If I can get some covering fire I believe I can make a run for it," answered Chen.

"Will do. Walker and I will provide it. On *three*, run for it. *One… Two… Three…* GO!"

Walker and Sergeant White opened fire from the statue onto the nearest hostiles. Chen jumped up to his feet and began running for dear life toward the Bradley. A hostile caught sight of what was taking place and began shooting at Chen. A bullet from the hostile's automatic weapon caught Chen in the back of his neck. Chen hit the ground grasping at the wound. Chen, trying to apply pressure on his wound, coughed up blood, and began to die a slow, painful death in the middle of the courtyard.

"Chen!" Bronson yelled after witnessing what had happened from the first-floor building window.

Bronson shattered the window with the butt of his automatic rifle and began recklessly shooting at the hostile who had shot Chen. Engulfed by his rage, Bronson was oblivious to the hostile that began to creep behind him. The hostile stepped slowly, confident of his kill to come. The hostile pulled out a steak knife from his side waistband and became in reach of Bronson. The hostile unknowingly stepped on a piece of glass, which let off a loud crunch, from the window from which Bronson had broken. Bronson whipped the assault rifle 180 degrees toward the hostile and let off a full clip into the sternum of the hostile.

———

Smalls and Peña ran up to the second floor of the building. Smalls took the west wing toward the kitchen, and Peña took the east. Smalls inched his head out from behind the wall to look through the kitchen window. He could see hostiles running into the building where Bronson, Hawkins, and Anderson were. Smalls began shooting in small bursts at the hostiles.

"Be aware, Privates Bronson and Anderson, you have company on your asses," Smalls said over the walkie.

Peña rested his assault rifle on the sling Chen had made for his wounded arm. Peña pulled the shades clean off from the bedroom window and could see hostiles in the farmers' market using women and children as shields.

"Hawkins we have hostiles in the farmers' market with human shields. I could use some help over here," asked Peña over the walkie.

"Got it," replied Hawkins.

———

Hawkins turned his rifle toward the farmers' market and could see hostiles gripping women and children by the neck, using them as human shields. One by one, Hawkins began clearing out the farmers' market of hostiles. Women and children began scattering, screaming hysterically for safety. A hostile with a rocket launcher, on the north side of the courtyard, saw Hawkins taking out his brothers with ease. The hostile readied himself and aimed his launcher in Hawkins's direction.

"Look out, Hawkins!" screamed Peña into the walkie.

Before Hawkins had time to react, the hostile squeezed the trigger and the rocket shot across the courtyard toward Hawkins. With a loud explosion and debris falling from the top of the building, Hawkins was no more.

———

"What the fuck was that!?" Anderson yelled.

Anderson ran up the stairs where Hawkins was, only to discover the third-floor ceiling was blown clean off. Anderson ran back down the stairs and saw two hostiles running up the stairs toward him. Anderson shot at both hostiles and killed them instantly. Anderson continued down to the first floor to see Bronson covered in blood and hypnotized by his kill. Anderson walked over and slapped Bronson across the face.

"Let's go!" screamed Anderson.

Both Sergeant White and Walker were pinned downed behind the statue. Walker could see that the hostiles had begun to spread out and close in on their position. Walker shot off the last rounds in his clip and realized he had one magazine left. He discharged the magazine to the ground and replaced it with the fresh one.

Walker turned over to Sergeant White. "Sir, I'm down to my last magazine and these fuckers are determined to get that briefcase from us."

"I'm down to my last as well, private. We must get out from behind this statue or we're done for," replied White.

"We are going to need some cover fire," White said over the walkie.

"*Understood, Sir*" came the voice of Corporal Smalls.

"*On my mark, give them all you got, soldiers!*" barked Smalls.

"*FIRE!*" yelled Smalls.

The brigade let off a wave of fire from all directions. Smalls and Peña fired upon the nearest hostiles from the second-floor windows of the bedroom and kitchen. Bronson and Anderson began to shoot at the unsuspecting enemies from the first-floor window and front door.

"If you're planning on moving, gentlemen, now would be the time," suggested Smalls.

Sergeant White grabbed hold of the silver briefcase with his left hand and his pistol with his right. Walker followed suit, firing bullets toward the hostiles who were closest to the statue. Walker ran toward the Bradley, and White parted ways toward the nearest Hummer. Walker jumped onto the gunner and cocked the side hammer. The sound of the M242 chain gun being readied halted all the hostiles in their tracks. Walker let off a loud war cry and squeezed the trigger on the M242 chain gun. Walker pointed the gun to the adjacent hostiles. The hostiles were no match for the power of the chain gun bullets, which left holes the size of golf balls in the enemy, some left dead with limbs severed. The hostiles' numbers were cut in half within seconds. Two hostiles took refuge behind the statue in the center of the town and began to shoot at Walker. Walker ducked behind the chain gun and turned the gun toward the hostiles hiding behind the statue. Chunks of white clay fell off the statue as Walker began to drill the ammunition of the chain gun into the base of the nine-foot monument.

The hostile with the rocket launcher revealed himself once more and set his eyes on Walker. Peña caught sight of the hostile looking for an easy kill and began shooting in the hostile's direction. Peña shot the hostile in his left leg, which gave the hostile an awkward lean. Peña shot again and caught the hostile in his hip. The hostile fell forward and in the process of trying to catch himself from falling headfirst, squeezed the trigger of his rocket launcher. The rocket ejected from the launcher and sped off across the courtyard. The rocket made impact with the two hostiles hiding behind the statue. Flesh and bone painted the ground. The statue then began to rock and fall like a sawed-down redwood, crushing the remains of the two hostiles. Peña then finished off the rocket-wielding hostile with a bullet to the ribs.

—

The two hostiles tied up in the Hummer became extremely nervous with all the commotion that surrounded the vehicle.

Out of wanting to free themselves, the hostiles uncovered their faces and began to fiddle with the door handle. Both hostiles jumped out the back of the Hummer and ran as fast as they could away from the military vehicles. Anderson saw the escapees on his three and shot the tailing hostile right in the back. He then moved the rifle in the direction of the other hostile. The hostile turned his head to see his partner laid face first on the ground. Anderson saw the hostile's face, the same hostile who previously had been staring viciously at him through the rearview mirror of the Hummer, and shot him in the face.

"We are all clear, Sir," Smalls said over the walkie.

The remaining soldiers regrouped at the center of the courtyard. Sergeant Marcus White walked over and knelt over the body of Private Andy Chen. Chen lay dead with his eyes open toward the sky, hands still wrapped around his throat. White placed his hand over Chen's eyes to close them removed Chen's arms from his throat and placed them onto his chest. He then reached into Chen's shirt and removed his dog tags.

White put the dog tags in his side pouch and walked back over to the convoy.

"I want to know what we are fighting for, and what is more important than the lives of good soldiers," White said outspokenly.

Sergeant Marcus White laid the silver briefcase on the ground before him, flipped the latches and raised the top half of the briefcase open, revealing a total of five large folders stamped with "**TOP SECRET**" in bold lettering. Sergeant White took them out of the briefcase and handed them to his squad. Another folder sat in a netted pocket in the upper half of the briefcase. Sergeant White pulled it out from its pocket and read what was on the cover. "WEAPONS OF MASS DESTRUCTION."

"What is all of this?" White said while scanning through the documents.

"Looks to me like targeted cities back home," said Walker.

"New York, Los Angeles, Boston. All major cities with full, detailed information on potential bomb locations," Bronson added.

"Are they planning on killing Americans? Our own government?" questioned Peña.

"That's what it looks like to me. It's clear as day. Our government had us meet up with the biochemist and pick up a briefcase full of city locations and weapons blueprints that could destroy whole cities. We lost two brothers on this mission to retrieve something that's going to kill millions of our own people. We can't hand this over, Sir. We can't give up this information," argued Anderson.

"Well that's one thing we can finally agree on, Anderson," replied White.

"I can't let you do that, Sir," Corporal Calvin Smalls said while pulling out his sidearm and pointing it at his comrades.

"What you think you're doing Corporal?" White questioned.

"I have my own set of orders and it does not include destroying those documents. Now put them back in the briefcase and hand it here," demanded Smalls.

"He's bluffing," Bronson said while stepping forward.

"Try me." Smalls pulled back the hammer to his .45 Beretta.

"Why are you doing this?" asked White.

"The Company has its own agenda, and I'm stuck between a rock and a hard place," replied Smalls.

Smalls reached into his side pouch, pulled out a satellite phone, clicked *dial*, and pressed it to his face.

"Listen I have the briefcase in my possession. Come and pick me up," Smalls said.

"I can't let you do this," barked White while reaching for his Beretta.

Corporal Smalls opened fire and shot Marcus White in the thigh. Sergeant White fell to his hands and knees. Anderson, enraged, leaped at Smalls. Smalls opened fire again and Anderson took two to the chest. Anderson grabbed hold of Smalls and used his momentum to bring Smalls down underneath him. Both Bronson and Peña jumped on Smalls and Anderson. Bronson ripped the gun from Smalls's hand. Walker rolled over Anderson on his back, two visible bullet wounds entered Anderson's chest, and his eyes were slowly beginning to drift away, blood began to flow from his mouth down the side of his face.

"Sarge!" Anderson called out, coughing up blood.

"I'm here, Anderson." Sergeant White knelt before Anderson.

"Did I stop him?" asked Anderson.

"Yes, you did. Bronson has a hold of him."

"That's good" *cough* "Sarge… You know I never meant to be the black sheep of the group… It's been a pleasure serving under you, Sir."

"The pleasure was all mine… Private First Class Charles Anderson," White replied while holding Anderson's hand.

Anderson smiled and closed his eyes, the grip from his hand weakened, and his breath gave way. An eerie silence fell upon the convoy. Sergeant White reached into

Anderson's shirt and removed his dog tags. Walker sat there in shock still in disbelief of the cost of betrayal. So much death had surrounded him since the start of the mission. The feeling overwhelmed him with the sight of someone he knew dying in his arms. As Walker drifted back into reality he felt more anger than grief.

"Why the fuck you got to go be a hero, you racist bastard!" Walker said, shedding a tear.

"I warned him! This would have gone smoothly if he didn't be a hero. Fuck him. I never did like the racist prick anyway." Smalls said angrily.

"Shut up!" Bronson said while right hooking Smalls in the mouth.

Sergeant White removed his pants belt and wrapped it around his thigh to stop the bleeding. White stood up on his two feet under his own will, leaned forward, and picked up the briefcase. He glanced over at Anderson's body and knew it was time to move fast.

Chapter IV

Hafa Al Batin

1700 hours

"We got to move, and move fast," White suggested.

"What are we doing with this trader?" Bronson asked.

"Bring him, we need answers and I believe the people he works for are on their way. Walker, you ride with me. Bronson and Peña, take the Bradley. Gather any spare ammo and weapons. We leave in two minutes. And you, you slimy bastard, you're riding with me," White said to Smalls.

——

The remaining convoy packed and loaded the two vehicles. Walker took the driver's seat of the Hummer and White loaded Smalls into the backseat. Peña decided to take the wheel of the Bradley and Bronson stood at the gunner with a watchful eye toward any unexpected trouble they might encounter. Peña then honked the horn of the Bradley signaling they were ready to move. Walker and Peña then hightailed out of Hafa Al Batin.

———

"Is there anything you'd care to explain to me?" Sergeant White questioned Smalls.

"Like what?"

"Well for one, who are you working for? Because I know my own superiors wouldn't send one of my own men to take me at gunpoint."

"They call themselves 'the Company.' That's all they told me."

"Why would this 'Company' give you orders to make sure we deliver this briefcase back to base?"

"These two men came to my home two days before I departed. They knew everything, my financial problems, my house having a lean on it. They even knew my wife was four months pregnant. They made me a deal. A fresh start. All they asked was the retrieval of those documents. I was desperate."

"Come in, Sarge," Bronson called over the radio.

"Go ahead Bronson," White replied.

"We have a chopper on our six."

Sergeant White looked into his side view mirror and could see a helicopter gaining on the convoy: a jet black Sikorsky CH-53E Super Stallion. The Super Stallion is one of the largest helicopters in the United States's long list of aircrafts. Able to carry 37 troops, two pilots, and three gunners— one on either side and one on the tail—and with .50 caliber M2 machine guns, it is a force to be reckoned with. As large as the aircraft is, its maximum speed is 196 miles per hour. The sergeant knew he couldn't out run this helicopter.

"We can't stop, Sarge. If we do, they'll get a hold of the documents," Walker informed White.

"They're on our tail, Sir," Peña reported to White.

The Super Stallion continued to catch up to the convoy. Within minutes the helicopter was within 300 yards and closing in. The satellite phone in Smalls's side pouch began to ring. White turned back toward Smalls and reached for Smalls's side pouch. He grabbed the phone, pressed talk, and pressed the phone to his ear.

"This is Sergeant Marcus White of the United States Army. To whom am I speaking?"

"That is not important, Sergeant White. What *is* important is the contents of that briefcase. I want it now. You can hand it over or we can take it from you."

"Well there is a slight problem with that. The documents were destroyed in a firefight in Hafa Al Batin."

"Don't fuck with me, Mr. White. Stop your vehicles or we will stop them for you."

"That's *Sergeant* White to you, schmuck." White hung the phone up and tossed it to the backseat.

"I don't believe that was a good idea. These people mean business," Smalls said.

"I'm not going to be a part of killing millions of Americans. If I can prevent that, my mission is successful," replied White.

Sergeant White picked up the radio and called to the Bradley. "Listen up. The men on that chopper are determined to get their hands on these documents. By any means, we cannot let them have them. Bronson, if we are fired upon, rip them a new one."

"Understood, Sir." Bronson reloaded the gunner on the Bradley and pointed the chain gun at the helicopter.

The manned gunners directed their heavy machine guns at the Bradley. Instantaneously, the side gunner opened fire onto the Bradley. The sound of thunder came from the machine guns and shells rained upon the earth. Bullets hit the side of the Bradley. Bronson replied back with the spitfire of the chain gun. Bullets from the chain gun hit the gunner in his upper shoulder and chest. The gunner fell 200 feet out the chopper and hit the ground with a loud thump. A second gunner jumped on the machine gun and continued the assault. The chopper came full circle in front of the brigade and opened fire from its gun at the tail of the helicopter.

———

Sergeant White grabbed hold of Walker's assault rifle and inched his way out the passenger window of the speeding Hummer. White opened fire at the underbelly of the Super Stallion with no effect. The gunner refocused his attention from the Bradley to the front of the Hummer. Walker swerved the vehicle from left to right to avoid being shot at.

"Try and keep this baby stable," yelled White.

———

With the gunner preoccupied with the Hummer, Bronson aimed the chain gun at the rear propeller and squeezed the trigger. The bullets tore viciously through the rear propeller like famished dogs. Smoke began to appear from the propeller, it decelerated to a screeching halt and the chopper had no way of turning fast enough to avoid the continued abuse from the Bradley's chain gun. Bronson sprayed more ammunition into the chopper and hit the main propeller. The Super Stallion began to spin and descend dangerously fast. Unable to control the chopper the Stallion made a destructive landing on the side of a sandy hill. Parts of the chopper littered the ground. A small fire broke out at the rear of the helicopter. Suddenly a man in a torn-up dark suit covered in blood and dust crawled his way out of the chopper. In his hand he carried a satellite phone. He pressed it to his ear.

"Pick up was unsuccessful. I repeat, mission is a failure. Send in the night seekers," the unknown man said with his last breath.

———

The brigade drove to the wreckage eager to find answers. Bronson kept the chain gun trained on the remains of the helicopter waiting on any hostile movement. Both Walker and White exited the vehicle with assault rifles hugged up against their chests as they made their way closer to the wreckage. Peña followed suit exiting the Bradley with his hand glued to his assault rifle, taking no chances of being shot in the back. White knelt before the body of the suited man. White began to examine the limp body, searching for any form of identification, but there was nothing. No I.D., no dog tags, nothing. White pulled the phone from the grip of the dead man, pressed call, and pressed the phone to his face. Two rings went by before someone picked up but no one spoke on the opposite line.

"This is Sergeant—" but the phone conversation was cut short before Sergeant White could finish what he was saying.

Both Peña and Walker stepped into the helicopter looking for anything to salvage. Peña walked into the cockpit to see both pilots dead, their bodies fused with the metal of the helicopter. They had endured the full force of the crash. Walker searched the remainder of the helicopter to find a gunner mangled by a piece of steel from the interior of the chopper and another burned to a crisp by the fire at the rear of the aircraft.

"What did you find in there?" White yelled out.

Both privates stepped out from the side of the helicopter. "We found some ammo, a pistol, a first aid kit, and two pairs of night vision goggles."

"Good. Load it up. We are running out of daylight. And we must keep moving. They will eventually come looking for their comrades."

"What do we do now, Sergeant?" Peña questioned.

"We must get back to Kuwait City. I have a trustworthy friend that can get this intel to the right people and expose this 'Company.' The American people must know what is really going on."

———

The convoy loaded up the spare ammunition and made their way to Kuwait City. The sun began to descend behind the sandy mountains. The convoy had now met a new enemy, an enemy that spoke the same dialect as them. An enemy that had manipulated one of their own and now wanted blood.

Chapter V

Far East of Hafar Al Batin

2000 hours

Night fell upon the convoy. The warmth from the sun quickly turned into a chill from the night breeze. The fire from the helicopter crash was now a mere speck in their rearview mirrors. The heat rising from the Hummer's front lights made it evident that it was way below 60 degrees. The four remaining Spartans and their newly acquired prisoner were what remain of a squad of eight. There had been enough bloodshed and lives lost over these documents, and they all knew it. But what was much more important to them was the future lives that would be lost if these documents were to reach the hands of the Company. The sergeant had the full cooperation of his privates, and they were ready to walk through the gates of hell with him if need be.

"We will camp out tonight. We are in need of some rest. We will pull off road for about a quarter mile and make camp," White informed Peña.

"Copy that, Sir," Peña replied.

Walker led the Bradley off the main road and drove about a quarter mile into the desert. The convoy finally came to a stop, and Walker and White exited the Hummer. Bronson and Peña stepped out of the Bradley as well.

"This is as good as it's going to get. Let's make camp," White instructed.

——

Walker began the campfire and Peña jumped onto the Bradley and started handing Bronson rations and a couple of blankets. Sergeant White walked to the back of the Hummer and led Smalls out of the vehicle and sat him by the campfire.

"Are we going to have a problem?" White asked Smalls.

"No, Sir."

The convoy surrounded the fire and embraced its warmth. Bronson began to clean his assault rifle and reload his magazine one bullet at a time. Walker took out his wallet from his back pocket, pulled out some family photos, and began to reminisce about the good times and remember why he was in the army. Peña placed one of the night vision goggles on his head that he'd confiscated from the helicopter, and began to examine the other night vision goggle. Sergeant White took out his Beretta from its holster and began to stare at the engraved letters on the handle.

"What does that say, sergeant, if you don't mind me asking?" asked Smalls.

"Loyalty, above all else," replied White.

"That means your bitch ass," Peña said under his breath.

"Fuck you, Francis. I had my reasons. If you were in my shoes, you would do the same," barked Smalls.

"That's enough with the shit talking from you two." White turned his attention to Walker. "Walker is that your family? Why are you out here and not with them?"

"Yes it is, Sir. In this picture are my grandmother, mother, and I. My mother died when I was young, and my father, well I never had the chance to know him. My grandmother took me in and raised me. Times have been tough, so I enlisted in the army to help her out. In the beginning I thought it was a mistake, seeing how things have been unraveling, but I'm glad I did. You guys have been the brothers I never had. Do you have any family, Sarge?"

"Yes I do. Two beautiful women wait for me back in Richmond, Virginia. Veronica, my wife, and Crystal, my daughter. I do this for them. I want to see my daughter have a bright future, which is why I am determined to get these documents into the right hands."

"What about you Francis? Have anyone back at home waiting on you?" asked Walker.

"Yes. My senorita Anna-Marie and my son, Francisco. Before I left home, my wife was pregnant with our second son."

"Just like you Puerto Ricans. Bunch of jackrabbits, spitting kids out like sunflower seeds," laughed Bronson.

"Ha! Kiss my ass. At least I can have kids, Mr. Spit Blanks," laughed Peña.

"Hey, no need to get personal," laughed Bronson.

"So you have no one waiting in Boston for you, Bronson?" asked Walker.

"Yes, I do. My girlfriend Rebecca. We been together for two years," replied Bronson.

"And have you told her you been cheating with her with the weight machine? Look at your arms bro. Pump anymore iron you'd be shitting diamonds," joked Peña.

"I am a bit diesel, huh?" Bronson squeezed Peña's wounded arm.

"Let go!" Peña pulled away in agony.

Smalls stood up. "You see, I know for a fact that if any of you were in my shoes, you would have done the same exact thing for your family."

"That's true, but the difference is none of us would have shot one of our own," replied White.

—

After White replied to Smalls's remark, the privates fell silent and put their heads down remembering what they had gone through. Smalls opened his mouth to speak but nothing came out but a gasp for air. Smalls reached and grabbed hold of his chest. Blood dripped from his hands and he fell to his knees. Smalls removed his hands from his chest and looked at his hands. At that moment another bullet entered his chest and Smalls fell sideways to the ground.

"We're under attack!" screamed Walker.

More shots were fired from the darkness of the desert.

"Ahh, I'm hit!" screamed Walker grabbing hold of his calf.

"I can't see shit. Its dark as fuck," yelled Bronson.

"Here, take this." Peña tossed a pair of night vision goggles to Bronson.

Peña pulled a pair of goggles over his eyes, as did Bronson. The night vision made it much easier to see in the dark. Peña saw that four unknown men dressed in full black uniforms, black masks, and night vision goggles surrounded them. They carried semiautomatic weapons, and seemed quite accurate with their shots. Both Walker and White dove, crawled between the Bradley and the Hummer, and reached the opposite side for safety. Bronson and Peña followed closely, shooting in small bursts at the four unidentifiable hostiles. Peña shot three bullets into the chest of one hostile. The hostile fell and became a problem no more. The hostile nearest to the fallen comrade let off a few rounds at Peña, nearly missing Peña's face and resting in the side of the Bradley. Peña rolled to his side and replied back with a couple of bullets to the hostile's sternum and shoulder. The hostile dropped and remained motionless. Bronson continued his defense, exchanging fire against the hostiles' offense. Bronson shot again and the bullets from his assault rifle connected with the enemy's shoulder and chest. Bronson then took cover behind the Bradley to replace his gun's empty magazine. Peña tossed Bronson a fresh clip, and Bronson inserted it into his gun.

Bronson then turned back toward the area where the hostiles had been shooting to be confronted face to face with the final hostile.

Bronson swung his rifle up with much force and knocked the hostile's weapon out his hands. The hostile reached, grabbed hold of Bronson's gun, and began to tug at it with all his might. Bronson released his right-hand grip from the gun and swung with all his might at the face of the enemy. The hostile stumbled back and Bronson lunged at him with a left hook to the body, then a right hook to the side of the face. The hostile fell on his back and Bronson pounced onto him. Bronson began repeatedly punching at his face. The hostile reached for Bronson's face but had no chance against the abuse he was receiving. The enemy finally stopped struggling but Bronson kept at it, blood dripping from Bronson's bare knuckles, as if he were numb to the pain of bone-on-bone contact. Sergeant White and Walker ran up behind Bronson, and each of them grabbed hold of Bronson's massive biceps and removed him from atop of the battered body. Walker looked over at the hostile Bronson had continuously struck with his fists. His face had been mutilated. Completely swollen, his left cheekbone caved in under the extreme force of fist-to-face brutality, the night vision goggles completely destroyed and embedded into the eye sockets of the hostile, blood spooling from his nose and mouth. This poor soul had no chance against Boston's high school wrestling champ.

"Snap out of it, private," White told Bronson.

"I'm good, Sir," responded Bronson.

"You done a serious number to that guy's face," Walker added.

—

"Look, we have a straggler," Peña pointed at the wounded hostile.

The convoy readied their weapons and sprinted toward the injured hostile. The enemy lay on his back. A bullet wound to his lower spine and hip prevented him from moving far. White kicked the gun further away from the hostile and crouched down beside him. White removed the goggles and mask off the hostile's face to the surprise of the comrades the hostile was… an American.

"Who do you work for? You're not wearing any military gear I can identify," asked White.

"Why should I tell you anything?"

"Because the way I see it, you're going to die a slow, painful death if we don't give you morphine to ease the suffering."

"Okay, okay. I work for an organization that calls themselves 'the Company.'"

"What is 'the Company'?"

"It's a private subcontractor, an organization that carries out certain operations the public eye would deem unconstitutional."

"What do they have planned for these documents?"

"I do not know, Sir. My orders were just to retrieve them."

"And my team, what does the Company plan to do with us?"

"Remove you permanently from the equation," the uniformed American began to choke on his blood and his body gave into the severity of his injuries.

"I guess we're dead any which way we put it, Sarge," Peña said.

"I guess so. The only way out of this is to reach my contact back at base. If we can make it there we'll be safe from the Company."

—

White ordered the remainder of his men to pack up and prepare to depart. White walked over to Smalls's body and turned him onto his back. He then reached into his shirt and pulled out Smalls's dog tags. White knew Smalls was a great soldier and, considering the circumstances Smalls was in, it would have made any soldier consider the decision he made.

The night came to a close and the convoy was approximately 80 miles from the city of Kuwait. The convoy had been beaten and battered, and with each fallen comrade, moral severely dropped. Low on ammo and rations, the convoy had to move much quicker. Their enemy was no longer the hostile natives of this country, but their own government.

Chapter VI

0700 hours

Morning came, and the temperature rose with the morning sun. Peña jumped into the driver's seat of the Bradley and Bronson sat on top of the monstrous vehicle with the chain gun at hand. Bronson began to squint at something not far off. He reached over for his binoculars and placed them over his eyes for a better view. With his newfound vision, he could see the black Hummer the four men came in on the previous night.

"Sarge, I found the vehicle these men came in on. It's about a mile from our position," Bronson informed White.

"Excellent. We'll seize it. We may be able to find something useful."

Walker and White jumped into the vehicle and followed Peña toward the black Hummer, their new prized possession.

The black Hummer looked well equipped, with exceptionally updated tracking equipment. A screen on the passenger seat was functional and displayed a map, with a blinking dot next to the location of the vehicle.

"What is that blinking red dot on the screen? Is that supposed to be our vehicle that's blinking?" Walker asked.

"But how you suppose they got a tracking device on one of our vehicles?" Bronson asked.

"Smalls," replied White.

Sergeant White walked back over to his vehicle and opened the Hummer's back passenger door. He looked around and saw the satellite phone on the floor of the Hummer and picked it up.

"This is how they have been tracking us all this time," White explained.

"Let's get rid of it now," Peña suggested.

"No, I have an idea. We may be able to use this to direct them away from the documents. They will be looking for our vehicles so we need someone to use their vehicle to drive to base and find Lieutenant Brown. Any volunteers?" White asked.

"Well I'm not skipping out of whipping some ass. I'm staying behind," answered Bronson.

"So am I, Sarge." Peña agreed with Bronson.

"I'll do it then Sarge. I'll deliver those documents. You can count on me," Walker said confidently.

"All right then. Take the briefcase. Bronson, Peña, give me your dog tags. I want you to make sure the dog tags of our brothers make it to their family."

"Got it, Sarge."

Sergeant White handed Walker six dog tags and the briefcase. He then saluted Walker, about-faced, and walked to the Hummer. Bronson and Peña stepped toward Walker.

"Good luck. You have more heart than you give yourself credit for. Glad to call you my brother." Bronson saluted and walked toward the Bradley.

"Well, you know me. I'm no good at serious situations, so all I'm going to say is don't fuck this up. And I'll see you on the other side," Peña said, saluting and walking off toward the Bradley.

——

Sergeant White and Privates Bronson and Peña jumped into their vehicles and drove off into the opposite direction from Kuwait City. Walker stared at them driving off and had a strong gut feeling this would be the last time he saw any of them alive. Walker snapped back to the realization of how important his mission was, jumped into the black Hummer, and made his way to Kuwait City.

One hundred miles from Kuwait City

0900 hours

"I hope Walker is okay. He should be there soon," Peña said, breaking the awkward silence in the Bradley.

"I'm sure he'll be fine, I'm more concerned about us. With that tracking device we have, we might as well have a bull's-eye on our asses," Bronson replied.

"It's been several hours since we left Walker and still no sign of the Company. Do you think that satellite phone is even a tracking device?"

"Don't speak so soon Francis. We have the Company on our six."

"Come in, Sarge. We have the Company on our tail. Two Hummers and an AH-64 Apache helicopter packing some serious firepower."

"Copy that, Bronson. Time to put on a show. Give em' hell," replied White.

———

Bronson turned the chain gun toward the Company vehicles. He pulled out his black bandana from the belt loop of his pants and wrapped it around his head. He then pulled back the recoil and waited until the helicopter came close enough for a clear shot. The helicopter came in range and Bronson released the firing power upon the helicopter. The helicopter maneuvered out the way of the oncoming bullets and returned fire of its own. The helicopter, equipped with armor-piercing bullets, shot at the Bradley, hitting the side and puncturing its armored plates. Bronson swung the chain gun to his right and continued to shoot at the helicopter. A hundred rounds a minute shot into the sky. The helicopter's maneuvering capabilities were faster than Bronson's aiming speed. The helicopter moved to the left and opened fire again hitting the chain gun and Bronson in the shoulder. Bronson fell into the Bradley's cockpit, grabbing hold of his shoulder.

"Are you hit!?" Peña yelled.

"Just drive this shit," Bronson yelled back.

Bronson climbed back up to see the chain gun damaged from the helicopters assault.

"Shit," Bronson said angrily.

Bronson stepped back into the Bradley and grabbed hold of his assault rifle and a pair of grenades. Bronson stepped back out of the Bradley and saw one of the Hummers inching its way to the side of the Bradley. Bronson shot at the Hummer and the Hummer pulled back. Bronson returned his attention back to the helicopter and opened fire once more. Bronson had a better maneuvering capability but less of an impact with the assault rifle's bullets. He continued shooting and caught the underbelly of the helicopter. The helicopter then pulled back and the Hummer pulled up beside the Bradley. A uniformed man pulled out a submachine gun out the window and shot Bronson twice in the side of his ribcage. Bronson clutched his side and fell back into the Bradley screaming in agony. Peña turned the wheel hard to his right and slammed the Bradley into the Hummer, crushing the arm of the man between the vehicles and sending the Hummer out of control off the road. The

Hummer collided with a huge boulder, leaving the Hummer out of commission, severely damaged.

"Speak to me, Bronson! Don't fucking die on me!" Peña yelled.

"Sarge, come in. Bronson has been hit."

"Copy that. Pull up in front of me. I'm going to see if I can hold them off."

Peña pulled up ahead of the Hummer and White saw that the other Hummer began to pull up behind them. White reached for his pouch and pulled out a couple of grenades. White pulled the pins and threw the grenades out the window. The grenades exploded 10 feet from the enemy's Hummer and forced them to slow down to avoid being another casualty. The helicopter then pulled ahead of the Bradley, shooting at the front of the vehicle and in turn hitting the engine, forcing a violent stop. White had no time to react and smashed the Hummer into the back of the Bradley.

———

Both the Bradley and Hummer stood motionless. The Company's helicopter circled the wreckage and descended for a landing 20 feet from where the soldiers' vehicles stood motionless. Two men exited the helicopter and four exited the Hummer. Two of the men grabbed hold of the disoriented Sergeant White and pulled him from the Hummer. They disarmed White and threw him to the ground.

"Check the Bradley. Make sure no one is alive," ordered the leader of the group.

—

Peña reached for his assault rifle and waited for the Company personnel to step in unexpectedly. One of the men stepped down from the ladder from the rooftop into the Bradley and crouched down to check Bronson's pulse.

"The big guy is down," yelled the unsuspecting Company personnel.

The man then turned around and saw Peña crouched by the driver's seat with his assault rifle pointed at him. Before the man could utter a word Peña shot him dead.

"We have a live one," yelled one of the company personnel standing on top of the Bradley.

"Well, take him out. We have no use for him," replied the leader.

"Say goodnight, private," one of the personnel said before chucking a grenade into the Bradley.

Peña saw the grenade fall into the Bradley. He fell to his knees, grabbed hold of his rosary around his neck and kissed the wooden Jesus.

"Forgive me Lord" Peña said softly.

The fire from the explosion shot out the top of the Bradley. White punched the ground with his bare hands with anger.

"Now that we have your attention, where are my documents?" asked the leader.

"I don't have them."

"I see you're going to be difficult. Should we pay a visit to your wife and daughter?"

"Damn you. You leave them out of this. The documents aren't here."

"He's right boss. There's nothing in the Hummer," yelled a Company personnel searching in the Hummer.

"So where are they?"

White replied and spit blood on the uniform of the Company personnel. "They're in a safe place. Now you can go fuck yourself."

The Company personnel held Sergeant White's pistol in his hand and examined the engraved words on the handle.

"Loyalty huh? It costs more lives than it saves," the Company leader said.

The leader of the group pressed the barrel of the pistol to Sergeant White's forehead, pulled back the hammer and squeezed the trigger. Sergeant White's lifeless body fell over to its side. The Company personnel jumped back on their vehicles and left as quickly as they came.

Operation: Rebirth

City of Kuwait, Army Base
1000 hours

Walker made it to base with the briefcase at hand. Limping through the base, Walker got an eerie chill up his spine, the chill he always got when something bad had happened. Walker grabbed hold of his wounded leg and asked the nearest army personnel to escort him to Lieutenant Brown. Walker limped his way up to a man standing before a table in full uniform, with badges and footwear that looked freshly polished, looking at a large map of Saudi Arabia.

"Lieutenant Brown?" Walker asked.

"Yes." Brown redirected his eyes to Walker's.

"I was ordered by Sergeant Marcus White to hand this briefcase over to you. He said you would know what to do with it."

"He did, did he? Seeing that he did not hand this to me personally suggests something went wrong."

"I don't believe he survived the mission. My whole brigade died protecting that briefcase, people I called brothers. Please see that the right thing is done with the contents of that briefcase," Walker said, collapsing to the floor.

"Get this soldier medical attention now!" Lieutenant Brown ordered.

——

Walker awoke in a hospital bed and stood staring at the ceiling, relieved that he had accomplished his mission. A white gown covered Walker's otherwise naked body, and an intravenous tube supplied pain-relieving medication directly into his bloodstream. A doctor entered the room with a clipboard and a syringe.

"Hey, doc. Do you know if anyone from my unit showed up to base?"

"No. I believe none have arrived."

"Oh. How am I doing?"

"You are going to be just fine."

The doctor removed the cap from the syringe and inserted the needle into Walker's intravenous tube.

"Whoa. I'm feeling real tired all of the sudden. What did you do to me?" Walker asked nervously.

"It's something to help you sleep."

"But I'm not tired."

"Oh, you will be. My boss wanted to thank you for returning our documents back to us. You did well Private Walker. We will make sure you have a proper burial."

"You, son of a bitch!"

"The more you struggle the faster you'll sleep."

"You won't get away with this!"

"On the contrary, we already have. You were the last loose end."

"I'll… get… you… for…"

Walker's breath gave out.

The doctor pulled out his satellite phone and pressed it to his ear.

"It's done, Mr. President."